Short Pants

A play based on a traditional folktale
by Kath Lock

Illustrated by Tracie Grimwood

Characters

Maybelle

Farmer

Storekeeper

Susannah

Annabelle

Peter

Narrator 3
(Storyteller)

Narrator 1
(Storyteller)

Narrator 4
(Storyteller)

Narrator 2
(Storyteller)

Turn to pages **21**, **22** and **23** for Sound and Stage Tips

Short Pants

Scene   The Farm Kitchen

(The family members are hard at work. The Farmer's wife, Maybelle, is decorating a cake. His sister, Susannah, is baking biscuits and scones. His daughter, Annabelle, is sewing roses onto her new dress. Peter, the Farmer's son, is polishing the harness for the horse he will ride in the parade.)

Narrator 1:   All of the farmer's family are preparing for the spring fair. The fair is on only once a year and everyone in the village is very excited.

Narrator 2: The villagers have been preparing for the competitions for many weeks by cooking …

Narrator 3: And making their finest handicrafts.

Narrator 4: They have been looking after their most beautiful plants and protecting them from the frost …

Narrator 1: And washing and brushing their finest animals.

Narrator 2: There will be parades and balloons and rides.

Narrator 3: The carnival rides and sideshows have been set up.

Narrator 4: All the village children have been watching and waiting for them to be ready.

Farmer: I have the animals ready for tomorrow.

(He points to his patched and stained overalls.)

I think I'll go into town and buy a new pair of overalls. These aren't good enough to wear while I'm showing the animals.

Maybelle:	That's a good idea. You'll only be in the way here.
Annabelle:	We're all still getting ready.
Maybelle:	You do have a better pair of overalls, but no one has had time to wash them.
Susannah:	And I haven't had time to bake any bread or to prepare our tea. While you're in town would you buy some bread and something for us to eat, please?
Annabelle:	While you're there would you buy me some pink ribbon to go with these roses, please Dad?
Susannah:	I need some sticky labels to go on these plates of biscuits. You can buy them at the general store. Would you get me a dozen, please?
Peter:	I'm nearly out of polish, Dad. Would you find some for me at the saddlery, please?

Narrator 1: So the farmer wrote a list of all the things that his family wanted, and off he went to the village.

Narrator 2: First, he went to the saddlery and bought the polish.

Narrator 3: Then, he went to the general store to buy the sticky labels and some pink ribbon.

Narrator 4: Lastly, he went to the bakery to buy the bread.

Narrator 1: He wondered what he should buy for tea.

Narrator 2: He looked at the pies.

Narrator 3: They smelled delicious …

Narrator 4: No, they would be eating pies at the fair.

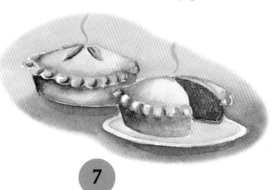

Narrator 1: Then, he saw a chocolate cake.

Narrator 2: That would be a nice surprise.
But what else could he buy?

Narrator 3: Fish and chips. Yes.
They all like fish and chips.

Narrator 4: But the fish and chip shop was closed
until 5 o'clock.

Narrator 1: So, he decided to buy his overalls first.

Storekeeper: Can I help you, farmer?

Farmer: Yes. I'm looking for a pair of overalls,
but I can't find the size I want.

Storekeeper: Mmmm, we've sold lots of overalls today.
You should have come in yesterday.
We had plenty then.

Farmer: Yesterday I didn't need them, but the
washing isn't done, so today I do.

Storekeeper: Well then, let's see what we can find
for you.

Narrator 2: The storekeeper held up many pairs
of overalls. Some were too short.

Narrator 3: Some were too long.

Narrator 4: Some were too large.

Narrator 1: Some were too small …

Narrators 1, 2, 3, and 4: And some of them were a very strange colour.

(Storekeeper holds up a pair of purple overalls with large yellow spots.)

Farmer: These won't do at all. Is that all that you have left?

Storekeeper: There's just one pair at the bottom of this box, but I'm sure they'll be too long for you. They're very strong, but they're last season's, so you can have them a bit cheaper.

Farmer: Too long doesn't matter. Someone will shorten them for me.

(He tries them on and they do fit, although they are too long.)

Farmer: I'll take them. If no one has time to take them up I can just fold up the bottoms and put a pin in them.

Narrator 1: So the farmer went home.

Narrator 2: He had been concentrating so hard on choosing his overalls that he had completely forgotten about the fish and chips for tea.

Narrator 3: His family would not be pleased. Thank goodness he'd remembered the bread and all of the other things that they wanted.

Narrator 4: As he walked into the kitchen he saw that they were all sitting at the table.

Narrator 1: When he looked around he saw that none of them had finished their competition entries. They were all talking at the same time.

Maybelle: Well, what did you get for our tea?

Susannah: I hope you didn't buy pies and pasties.

Annabelle: Did you bring some ice-cream for dessert?

Peter: I bet you bought fried rice again.

Farmer: Oh, bother and darnation! I forgot. I thought we'd have fish and chips, but the shop wasn't open.

(They all mutter and mumble and wag their fingers at him.)

Farmer: Never mind, I did buy the bread.
We can have jam and cream on it …
and I did buy this chocolate cake.

*(He pulls a chocolate cake out of his bag.
Everyone smiles.)*

You know, I couldn't even find a pair of
overalls to fit me.

Maybelle: Don't worry about your overalls now.
We're hungry and we haven't had a chance
to eat all day.

Narrator 2: So the farmer decided not to tell them
about his overalls just yet.

Narrator 3: Best to wait until they had eaten
and had a rest, he thought.

Narrator 4: The family ate the bread and jam,
the chocolate cake and some apples.
They were about to finish their decorating,
packing and polishing, when the farmer
announced …

Farmer: These are the overalls that I bought, but they're about 15 cm too long. Maybelle, would you shorten them for me?

Maybelle: Any other night I would, but my eyes are so tired from doing all of this fine work on the cake. I just wouldn't be able to do it tonight.

Farmer: Susannah, could you shorten them for me?

Susannah: If you can wait until I find my specs, I'll gladly do them for you. I put them down somewhere and I can't see without them.

Farmer: But I need to wear these overalls tomorrow. What about you, Annabelle? Can you help me?

Annabelle: Sorry Dad. I still have to wash my hair and clean my shoes.

Farmer: Peter, could you do it?

Peter: Not tonight, Dad. I still have to clean out the horse trailer.

Farmer: Oh well, I'll just fold them up and put some pins in them for tomorrow.
They can be sewn some other time.

(The family all go to sleep in their beds.)

Narrator 1: The farmer sighed and went off to bed, but he woke up suddenly at eleven o'clock.

FX: *(Clock strikes eleven.)*

Narrator 1: When he couldn't go back to sleep he decided to shorten his overalls.

(Farmer stretches and yawns as he climbs out of bed.)

Narrator 2: The farmer crept out of bed, went to the kitchen and found a pair of scissors. He cut 15 cm off the bottom of the overalls and carefully stitched the hem.

(Farmer holds up the overalls and admires his sewing.)

Then he went back to bed.

Narrator 3: The clock struck midnight and it woke up Maybelle.

FX: *(Clock strikes twelve.)*

(Maybelle stretches and yawns as she climbs out of bed.)

Maybelle: It's only midnight, but I feel wide-awake. Perhaps I could take those overalls up and surprise my husband.

Narrator 4: Maybelle crept out of bed, went to the kitchen and found the scissors. She cut 15 cm off the bottom of the overalls and carefully stitched the hem.

(Maybelle holds up the overalls and admires her sewing.)

Then she went back to bed.

Narrator 1: The clock struck one o'clock and woke up Susannah.

FX: *(Clock strikes one.)*

(Susannah stretches and yawns as she climbs out of bed.)

Susannah: Now I'll never go back to sleep. Maybe I could shorten the overalls and it will surprise my brother when he puts them on.

Narrator 2: Susannah crept out of bed, went to the kitchen and found a pair of scissors. She cut 15 cm off the bottom of the overalls and carefully stitched the hem.

(Susannah holds up the overalls and admires her sewing.)

Then she went back to bed.

Narrator 3: The clock struck two o'clock and woke up Annabelle.

FX: *(Clock strikes two.)*

(Annabelle stretches and yawns as she climbs out of bed.)

Annabelle: Fancy my waking this early. I'll take up the hem of Dad's overalls. He will be surprised.

Narrator 4: Annabelle crept out of bed, went to the kitchen and found a pair of scissors. She cut 15 cm off the bottom of the overalls and carefully stitched the hem.

(Annabelle holds up the overalls and admires her sewing.)

Then she went back to bed.

Narrator 1: The clock struck three o'clock
and woke up Peter.

FX: *(Clock strikes three.)*

(Peter stretches and yawns as he climbs out of bed.)

Peter: I'm so excited about the fair that I'll never
go back to sleep now. Perhaps I could fix
Dad's overalls and surprise him.

Narrator 2: Peter crept out of bed, went to the kitchen
and found a pair of scissors. He cut 15 cm
off the bottom of the overalls and carefully
stitched the hem.

*(Peter holds up the overalls and admires
his sewing.)*

Then he went back to bed.

Narrator 3: The rooster crowed and the farmer's family tumbled out of bed.

Narrator 4: They were so excited that they were all talking at once.

(The Farmer stands and looks around.)

Farmer: Well, it's time for me to be getting ready to go. Will you be much longer? I'll just go and get dressed.

Narrator 2: The rest of the family stayed at the table, and each one of them looked very pleased.

Narrator 3: For they all knew that they had done something that would surprise him.

(The Farmer returns to the kitchen, wearing his VERY short pants!)

Sound and Stage Tips

About this play

This play is a story that you can read with your friends in a group or act out in front of an audience. Before you start reading, choose a part or parts you would like to read or act. There are eleven main parts in this play, so make sure you have readers for all the parts.

This play can easily have extra shopkeepers and villagers if you want to add more parts.

Reading the play

It's a good idea to read the play through to yourself before you read it as part of a group. It is best to have your own book, as that will help you too. As you read the play through, think about each character and how they might look and sound. How are they behaving? What sort of voice might they have?

Rehearsing the play

Rehearse the play a few times before you perform it for others. In *Short Pants* it is important to mime the actions, such as yawning, stretching, brushing the animals and cooking. Also, practise holding the overalls up high, so that the audience can see them.

Remember you are an actor as well as a reader. Your facial expressions and the way you move your body will really help the play to come alive!

Using your voice

Remember to speak out clearly and be careful not to read too quickly!

In *Short Pants*, the conversations between the characters are very important to the story.

Remember to look at the audience and at the other actors, making sure that everyone can hear what you are saying.

Creating Sound Effects (FX)

You will need a sound effect for a clock striking each hour after midnight. Use a gong, metallophone or something that makes a 'dinging' sound. Read the story to see if there are any other places in the play where you could add extra sounds.

Sets and Props

Once you have read the play, make a list of the things you will need. There are many little things you can make or collect for a performance of *Short Pants*. Here are some ideas to help your performance. You may like to add some of your own.

- Old pair of overalls
- Large pair of scissors
- Table for the farmhouse
- Baking tray
- Flour box
- Horse straps (strips of leather or plastic)

- Pot plants
- Five beds: tables or trolleys
- Sheet, blanket and pillow
- Checked cloth
- Toy animals
- Glasses or spectacles
- Measuring tape

- Simple tables or shopfronts with signs for:
  - Bakery
  - General Store
  - Fish and Chip Shop
  - Saddlery
- Chocolate cake
- Jar of jam
- Cream
- Bread baskets
- Long overalls
- Short overalls
- Funny pair of overalls or trousers with odd spots of colour
- Needlework or knitting
- Sewing needles and threads
- Clock

Costumes

This play can be performed using simple costumes that make the characters look like they live on a farm. It is set in the 'olden days', so think about the clothes that farm families might have worn. The Farmer needs to wear an old pair of tattered overalls! Remember that the Farmer's cut down overalls are a very important part of the story.

Have fun!

❖ Ideas for guided reading ❖

Learning objectives: prepare, read and perform playscripts; explore narrative order: identify and map out main stages of the story; practice using commas to mark grammatical boundaries (to aid reading); comment constructively on plays and performance, discussing effects and how they are achieved

Curriculum links: Mathematics: Measures, shape and space

Interest words: pants, harness, handicrafts, carnival, overalls, saddlery, storekeeper, hem

Resources: pencils and paper

Casting: (1) Narrator (2) Narrator 2 & Annabelle (3) Narrator 3 & Susannah (4) Narrator 4 & Peter (5) Farmer (6) Storekeeper & Maybelle

Getting started

- Read the title of the play and the blurb on the back cover. Ask the children to predict what the farmer's problem is, and what may happen in the play.

- Using the title, ask the children to decide where this traditional folktale may originate. Can they think of any other American words that are different to British words? (*pavement, sidewalk*)

- Look at pp2–3 together. Using the illustrations and the scene description, create voices for each character and narrator.

- Look at pp4–5 and draw attention to the use of ellipses (...). What effect does this have? (The pauses emphasise how long the villagers have been preparing.)

Reading and responding

- Explain that the role of the narrators is very important. Model reading the narrators' parts, using punctuation and expression to enhance the reading.

- As a group, read to p10. Praise good use of expression and punctuation.

- Ask the children to predict what may happen next in the story, giving reasons for their ideas. *Will someone shorten the farmer's overalls for him? Who?*

- Continue reading to p15. Ask them to revise their predictions for the rest of the play.

Archie the Big Good Wolf

A play by Allan Baillie

Illustrated by Betina Ogden

Collins

Characters

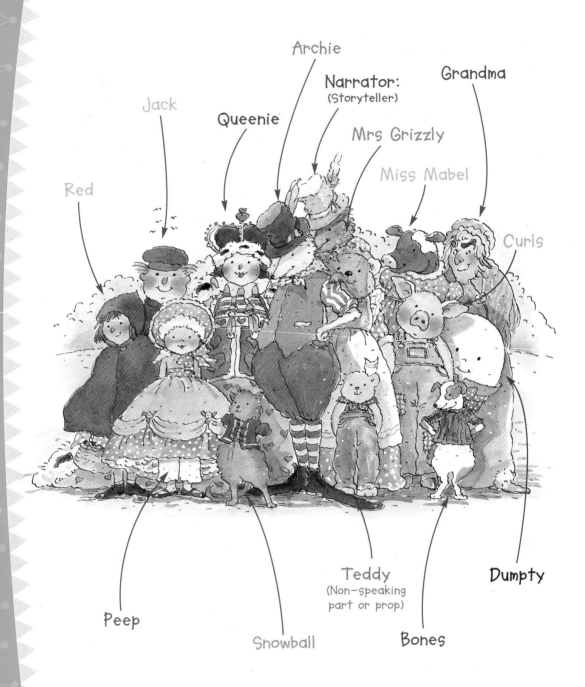

Archie

Narrator:
(Storyteller)

Grandma

Jack

Queenie

Mrs Grizzly

Miss Mabel

Red

Curls

Peep

Teddy
(Non-speaking
part or prop)

Dumpty

Snowball

Bones

Turn to page **29** for Sound and Stage Tips

Archie the Big Good Wolf

Scene 1

The Narrator sits on a chair, reading a Wolf book. He is wearing a hat and holding a piece of paper. A picture of Mother Goose is on a small table in the background. A large climbing plant sits on a window frame.

Narrator: *(Screwing up the paper and grimacing at the book.)* What …

(Looks up at the audience.)

Oh. Okay, okay, you found me. Yeah, I'm Archie the Wolf. And yeah, it's the Big, *Bad* Wolf, if you have to read the muck that that scrawny Mother Goose wrote about me.

(Throws the paper at the Mother Goose picture.)

So I'm supposed to be as nasty as a nest of wasps, right? Chasing pigs and chomping grandmas? Forget it, 'cause it just ain't so.

(Archie enters wearing a hat similar to the Narrator's hat. He tips his hat to the Narrator, who tips his own.)

Before I got stuck in this hole, I was the coolest guy in town.

(Archie mimes acting cool.)

It started on the day of Goldie's crime wave and that scribbler Mother Goose got *that* wrong too …

Scene 2

(In the corner there is a soft toy goose, or duck, wearing glasses. There is a painted brick wall, a toppled chair and a small bed with a rumpled blanket on it.)

Narrator: On that day, I'm just strolling around town, helping out as I go. Like I always do.

(Mrs Grizzly rushes in looking distressed. She is dragging a teddy bear.)
Suddenly Mrs Grizzly pokes her head out of the family mansion and screams.

Mrs Grizzly: Horrors! Someone's been sleeping in my enormously valuable antique bed! *(Pointing to the bed.)*

Narrator: So I get up there, moving faster than a speeding bullet.

(Archie runs on the spot, tips his hat to Mrs Grizzly, then sees the mess.)
I see that someone's gone wild in the house, bouncing about on the beds, breaking chairs and splashing food around everywhere.

Mrs Grizzly: *(Points at the teddy bear.)* Little Teddy's *terribly* expensive Ming porridge bowl is gone!

Archie: I'll get it back, lady. Don't you worry. Did anyone see anything?

Mrs Grizzly: Someone was lying on Teddy's bed, wasn't she?

(Looks at Teddy and makes Teddy nod in agreement.)
Yes, see? But she ran out of the house and round the corner.

Archie: Can you describe her?

Mrs Grizzly: (*Looks at Teddy.*) What do you think, Teddy? (*Mrs Grizzly looks up.*) Ghastly girl. She had awful yellow hair.

Archie: (*shocked*) Goldie?

Narrator: But I knew Goldie. She was a *sweet* girl who made me a toffee apple on my last birthday. It *couldn't* be her. Could it?

(*Archie turns away and Mrs Grizzly freezes.*) I hurry from the Grizzly family's mansion and look for clues.

Scene 3

(Queenie enters right with an empty tray. Archie moves towards her.)

Narrator: Round the corner I find Queenie Hart, looking very angry.

Archie: What seems to be the trouble, Queenie?

Queenie: The tarts!

(Queenie bangs her tray and shows the audience, hamming it up. Mrs Grizzly unfreezes and flips the straw side of the blanket over the box and changes the brick wall to the forest scene. She moves the chair to one side and then exits left.)

Archie: What tarts?

Queenie: The tarts! The tarts that I made. Lovely butterscotch tarts with raspberry jam. The best, the finest tarts in the country.

Archie: (*Squinting at the tray.*) Um, they're very nice.

Queenie: Idiot man! Goldie has stolen them away!

Archie: Oh. I'll look into it, Queenie.

(*Queenie freezes as Archie turns away.*)

Narrator: I see some birds pecking crumbs on the road and follow the trail.

Scene 4

(Peep enters left, sobbing loudly. She carries her shepherd's crook and a picture showing a couple of sheep.)

Narrator:	Out of town I find the Peep kid sitting on the grass and wailing.
	(Curls sneaks in from the right. Queenie unfreezes and helps him climb under the straw blanket before she exits right.)
Archie:	Hello, has Goldie been here?
Peep:	She snatches my crook and runs off!
Archie:	Which crook? *(Worried, looks around.)* How many gangsters do I have to chase now?
Peep:	It's not that sort of crook, dummy! *(Waves the picture and mimes the use of a crook.)* It is a shepherd's crook. I use it to pull the sheep in the right direction.
Archie:	Oh. And Goldie pinched it?
Peep:	It's worse than that.

Archie:	Really?
Peep:	I've got dumb sheep. Really dumb sheep. Because Goldie has my crook, those sheep think that Goldie is *me*. They've gone off with her!
Archie:	I'll find them, never fear. (*Turns from Peep and Peep freezes.*)
Narrator:	I set off again, looking for stray sheep.

Scene 5

(Curls is lying under the straw blanket with a cotton wool sheep nibbling the straw. Archie moves towards the blanket.)

Narrator: Soon I find a sheep nibbling at a moving pile of straw. I dig into the straw and pull out an old friend.

Archie: You all right, Curls?

Curls: *(Beats the ground in fury.)* No, I am *not* all right, Archie! This was my new house. Look at it now!

Archie: *(Investigates the blanket and helps Curls clamber to his feet.)*
It sure looks like a bad break and enter case to me.

Curls: Goldie did it! *(Stands up.)*

Archie: How'd she do it?

Curls: How? Well she started by saying that she would huff and puff and blow my house down unless I gave her my ancient and noble nose ring.

Archie:	And she did blow it down?
Curls:	Come on, Archie! She is only a girl!
Archie:	But … (*Waves his hand at the blanket.*)
Curls:	I laughed at her from the other side of my locked door. Goldie stamped her feet and tried to pull my house down with a long shepherd's crook. But that didn't work.
Archie:	But …

13

Curls: But her sheep pulled my house down!
(*Points at the sheep with a trembling finger.*)
Goldie points at my house and yells:
'Sick 'em guys!' And that whole mob of
vicious sheep charge at the house. The
door crashed down and then a wall and
then the roof. It was terrible.

Archie: It must have been nasty.

Curls: And she pulled the ring from my nose.
It hurt. (*Feeling his nose.*)

Archie: I'll get the ring back, somehow. (*Turns from
Curls and Curls freezes.*)

Scene 6

(Snowball, Bones and Miss Mabel enter left. Snowball holds a small branch against Miss Mabel as Bones pulls her. Miss Mabel is carrying a high moon.)

Narrator: I move on. Down the road Snowball and Bones are helping Miss Mabel down from a tree.

Archie: *(Helping Bones.)* Goldie was here, right?

(Curls unfreezes and flips the forest scene to the painted brick wall then exits right with the box.

Dumpty enters and sprawls on the blanket, beneath the brick wall.)

Snowball: Darling, it was absolutely awful! That blonde hussy trampled all over my tail. I screeched my fiddle.

Bones: Made Miss Mabel jump, it did. Jumped so high you wouldn't believe it.

Miss Mabel: And while I'm sitting up here, what do you think she went and did then, eh? Just ran off with my silver dish and spoon, that's all!

Bones: She's a thief!

Snowball: A thug!

Miss Mabel: A bandit!

(Bones, Snowball and Miss Mabel exit right. Archie walks slowly to Dumpty.)

Narrator:	I leave them, dragging my heavy feet along the trail. Goldie has changed from the sweet girl that I once knew into a wild hood. I can't understand it. Then I see a broken figure at the bottom of a high brick wall, moaning.

(Dumpty moans.) |
Archie:	You all right, Dumpty?
Dumpty:	She got me, Archie! I'm bound for the Great Frypan in the sky.
Narrator:	I see another of Peep's sheep near Dumpty.
Archie:	Goldie?
Dumpty:	*(coughs)* She snatched my hooded cloak …
Archie:	Yeah, she's become a bad egg.
Dumpty:	*(Shaking his head.)* But I grabbed her, Archie. I saw who she *really* was.

Archie: Hey! You mean Goldie ain't Goldie?

Dumpty: That's why she pulled me off the wall with a shepherd's crook. To stop me talking.

Narrator: Dumpty is cracking up.

Archie: Who is she, Dumpty?

(Dumpty coughs horribly, bangs his feet on the ground and throws his arms around.)

Narrator: But Dumpty's yolk has curdled.

(Dumpty's hand slides from a yellow wig. Archie stares at the wig, then turns to the audience and clicks his fingers.)

Of course! I leave him for Captain King's men to find and I race into the forest.

18

Scene 7

(Archie moves forward and talks to the audience.)

Archie: Someone's been pretending to be Goldie.

Narrator: Some tough crim, using Goldie's sweetness as a cover.

Archie: And I know who she is!

(Sticks up his thumb at Narrator who returns the gesture. Red enters left to the sound of sheep. She wears a riding hood and carries a basket and shepherd's crook. She sneers at the audience. Dumpty puts the blanket (blank side up) on the chair and exits right.)

Archie: Hello Red.

Narrator: I know Red from many police line-ups.

Red: What d'you want, Archie?

Archie: Where'd you get the riding hood, Red?

Red: This thing? I found it on a bush.

FX: (*Sheep baaing.*)

Archie: Where'd you get the sheep, Red?

Red: *Sheep*, Archie? What would I do with a
                 bunch of sheep? They've got nothing to do
                 with me.

                 (*She throws the crook offstage and the sheep
                 suddenly stop baaing.*)

Archie:	Where are you going, Red?
Red:	To Grandma's place. Are you gonna get in the way?
Archie:	What's in the basket, Red?
Red:	Flowers and jellybeans.
Archie:	For Grandma?
Red:	Sure.
Archie:	Let's look in the basket, Red.
Red:	(*Stepping back.*) You got a warrant, Archie? Get out of here.
Narrator:	I get out of here. Okay, I've got to get Red to show me the goodies before I can pounce. She knows this, so she won't let me look. But I have a plan …
	(*Archie wobbles his eyebrows at the audience. Red exits right.*)

Scene 8

(Grandma enters left, wearing fake glasses and a nightcap, and smoking a fake cigar. She goes to the chair, pulls it to the centre and sits with the blanket.)

Narrator: I run through the forest to Grandma's place so I can arrive before Red.

(Archie pants and runs on the spot. He takes a step towards the audience and lifts his hand to his mouth.)
Of course, you know that Grandma is a crook? Oh yes. Everyone knows she's an underworld 'fence'. You steal anything—anything *but* flowers or jellybeans—take it to Grandma's and she'll give you something for it.

(Archie moves towards Grandma and knocks on the non-existing door.)

Narrator:	I knock.
FX:	(*Knocking sounds.*)
	(*Grandma stands and places her blanket, nightcap and glasses on the chair.*)
Narrator:	Grandma comes to the door.
	(*Grandma puts the fake cigar in her mouth and pulls open the non-existing door between her and Archie. The door creaks.*)
FX:	(*Creaking sound.*)
Archie:	Hello Grandma, long time no see.
Grandma:	(*Jerks the cigar from her mouth.*) No, Archie.
Archie:	Quick, I got business.
Grandma:	Really? I got watches all over, and all in different times.
Archie:	But no business with you. (*Pushes Grandma towards left exit.*)

| Narrator: | This high-rise hole is like a castle. Nobody can find it, but here I'm a big wheel, a giant of business. Let that scribbler Mother Goose make a tale out of that! |

(Jack thrusts his face against the window.)

| FX: | *(Menacing music.)* |

Sound and Stage Tips

About This Play

This play is a story that you can read with your friends in a group or act out in front of an audience. Before you start reading, choose a part or parts that you would like to read or act. There are thirteen main parts in this play, so make sure you have readers for all the parts. Teddy could be either a prop or a non-speaking role.

Some readers could double up for some of the roles if you are working with a smaller group. Two people wearing black could help the actors move the props around the stage.

Reading the Play

It's a good idea to read the play through to yourself before you read it as part of a group. It is best to have your own book, as that will help you too. As you read the play through, think about each character and how they might look and sound. How are they behaving? What sort of voice might they have?

Rehearsing the Play

Rehearse the play a few times before you perform it for others. In *Archie the Big Good Wolf*, there are many scene changes. You will need to rehearse the stage directions carefully, as the action and dialogue move quickly from one character to another.

Remember you are an actor as well as a reader. Your facial expressions and the way you move your body will really help the play to come alive!

Using Your Voice

Remember to speak out clearly and be careful not to read too quickly! Try to capture the characters' voices. How does a dog sound, or a flying cow or a cracked egg? Archie's lines can be delivered in an unusual, first person, 'Private Detective' style. Remember to look at the audience and at the other actors, making sure that everyone can hear what you are saying.

Creating Sound Effects (FX)

Archie the Big Good Wolf is a terrific play for adding sound effects. Archie would love music! Try a private eye theme with dramatic highlights as he tracks the villain. The other characters could have their own pieces of music, too. Jack, for example, needs a very menacing theme.

There are plenty of opportunities for creative sound effects: the village noises before Mrs Grizzly's entrance, the birds pecking at Queenie's tart crumbs on the road, the forest and sheep sounds when Red appears, Jack breaking down the door and many more.

Sets and Props

Once you have read the play, make a list of the things you will need. Here are some ideas to help your performance. You may like to add some of your own.

- Two chairs
- Picture of Mother Goose
- Stuffed goose (or duck) with plastic glasses
- Fake window with a painted stone wall from the window to the floor
- Climbing plant
- Wolf book
- Two similar hats with a piece of paper stuck in one of them
- Painted brick wall with a forest scene painted on the other side
- Blanket, one side has a few straws and a cotton wool sheep painted on it
- Cardboard box bed
- Teddy bear (optional)
- Tray
- Picture showing Bo Peep with a couple of sheep

- Small branch
- Painted moon on a stick
- Yellow wig
- Red riding hood
- Shepherd's crook
- Fake cigar

- Covered basket—including a bowl, plate, spoon, tart and a large nose ring
- Fake glasses
- Nightcap
- A super exterminator!

Costumes

This play can be performed using simple costumes, to capture the idea of the characters. Similar hats for the Narrator and Archie, a bushy tail for Archie, brown gloves for Mrs Grizzly, hearts for Queenie, an eggcup for a hat for Dumpty and a bell for Mabel. Think about other ideas to help the audience work out the Mother Goose characters.

Have fun!

Ideas for guided reading

Learning objectives: prepare, read and perform playscripts: compare organisation of script with stories – how settings are indicated; define vocabulary in their own words; comment constructively on plays and performances, discussing effects and how they are achieved; use and reflect on some ground rules for dialogue

Curriculum links: Citizenship: People who help us – the local police

Interest words: antique, blond, hussey, the Great Frypan in the sky, reputation, Jack the Exterminator, menacing

Resources: whiteboard and pens

Casting: (1) Narrator (2) Archie & Bones
(3) Mrs Grizzly, Snowball & Red
(4) Queenie, Bones & Grandma
(5) Peep & Dumpty (6) Curls & Miss Mabel

Getting started

- Browse through the illustrations looking for familiar characters. Which other stories do they feature in? Chart stories and nursery rhymes.

- Read p4 to the children with expression. Discuss what kind of accent this might be read in (American). What clues are there that it might be American-English?

- Discuss unusual vocabulary, such as *scribbler Mother Goose, coolest guy* and work out the meaning by looking at the text. Can the group come up with alternative expressions?

- Draw children's attention to the scene descriptions immediately underneath scene titles. How do they help the reader?

Reading and responding

- Acting as *Narrator* yourself, encourage the children to read the other parts for scenes one and two. Discuss what might happen next and refer back to the text for clues.

- Encourage them to read on silently but hear each in turn. Prompt and praise for decoding of unknown words, e.g. *antique, reputation, menacing*.

- Choose parts for individuals and remind them to include stage direction, such as (*Dumpty moans*), p17

- Read through to the end together.